Freddy Fox

Story

&

Wildlife Photography

by
Ronald Meyer

NATURES BEAUTY PUBLISHING INC.

NATURES BEAUTY PUBLISHING INC.
Copyright 2004

Published by
NATURES BEAUTY PUBLISHING INC.
P. O. Box 725006
Berkley, Michigan 48072-5006
Voice: 248-546-0100
Fax: 248-399-3211
Email: BOOKS@NATURESBEAUTYPHOTOGRAPHY.COM

International Standard Book Number:
0-9754701-0-8
Printed in Hong Kong
First Edition   First Printing

Dedicated to

my

grandson

Theodore T. Watson

lovingly called

"Teddy Bear"

This is Freddy Fox.

Freddy is a baby Red Fox.

Freddy lives with his mother and father and sister, Frannie.

Freddy and his family
live in a warm and cozy den.
An old tree serves as a sturdy roof.

Freddy likes to sit in the doorway
and look at the big world outside his den.

As Freddy and Frannie get a little older, their mother lets them go out and explore. Mother tells them, "Have fun, but stay close to the den".

Freddy
likes to
climb.

Best of all,
Freddy likes to
play hide and seek
with Frannie. Young
foxes are shades of
gray in color so they can
hide easily. As Freddy grows he will
get a bright red coat and a big bushy tail.

Freddy's mother and father are good hunters. They bring home voles, rabbits, berries and other good food. Freddy's favorite is a fresh plump mouse.

One day, Freddy's father went to meet with other foxes to select a wise fox.

Freddy asked his mother; "When I grow up, what will I be? Will I be a wise fox?"

His
mother
answered,

"All foxes are
known to be sly.
To be wise, you
must learn from
the other animals."

"The Bear likes all types of meat. He is known for catching fish and eating them."

"To be healthy, the Bear knows he needs a balanced diet. He also eats fruits and vegetables. He is often seen eating berries."

His mother said,
"Eating the right foods
will help your body grow. But,
you also need to have food for your mind."

"The Bison understand the value of family. They watch over and care for their children."

"The Squirrel stores nuts all summer so it has food for the winter."

"The Mountain Goat knows to be careful and watch where it walks."

Then mother Fox said: "If you learn from all the animals, when you grow up

you will be the wise
old fox that lives on the
mountain of wisdom."